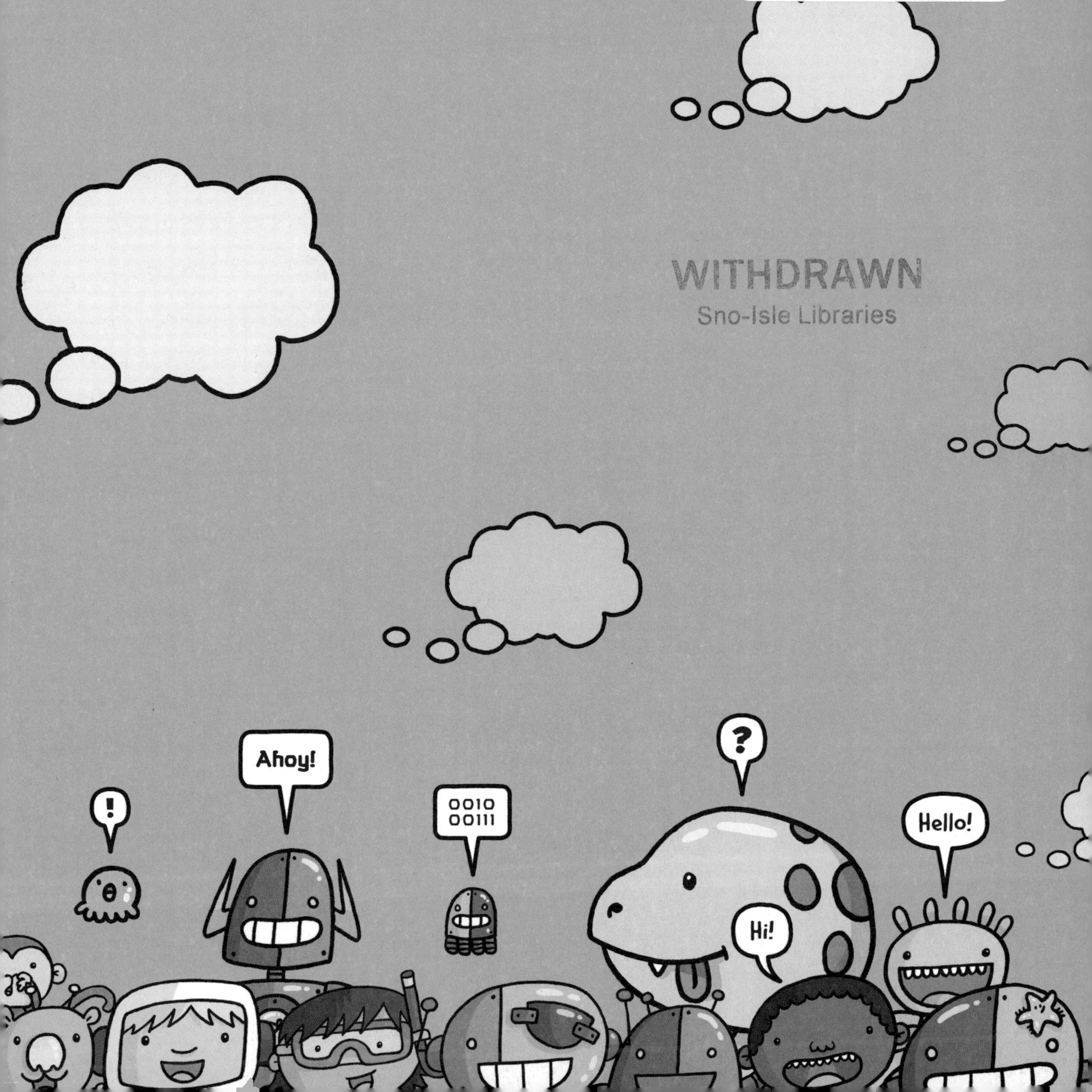
!
Ahoy!
0010
00111
?
Hi!
Hello!

# COMICS LAND

by
CAPSTONE

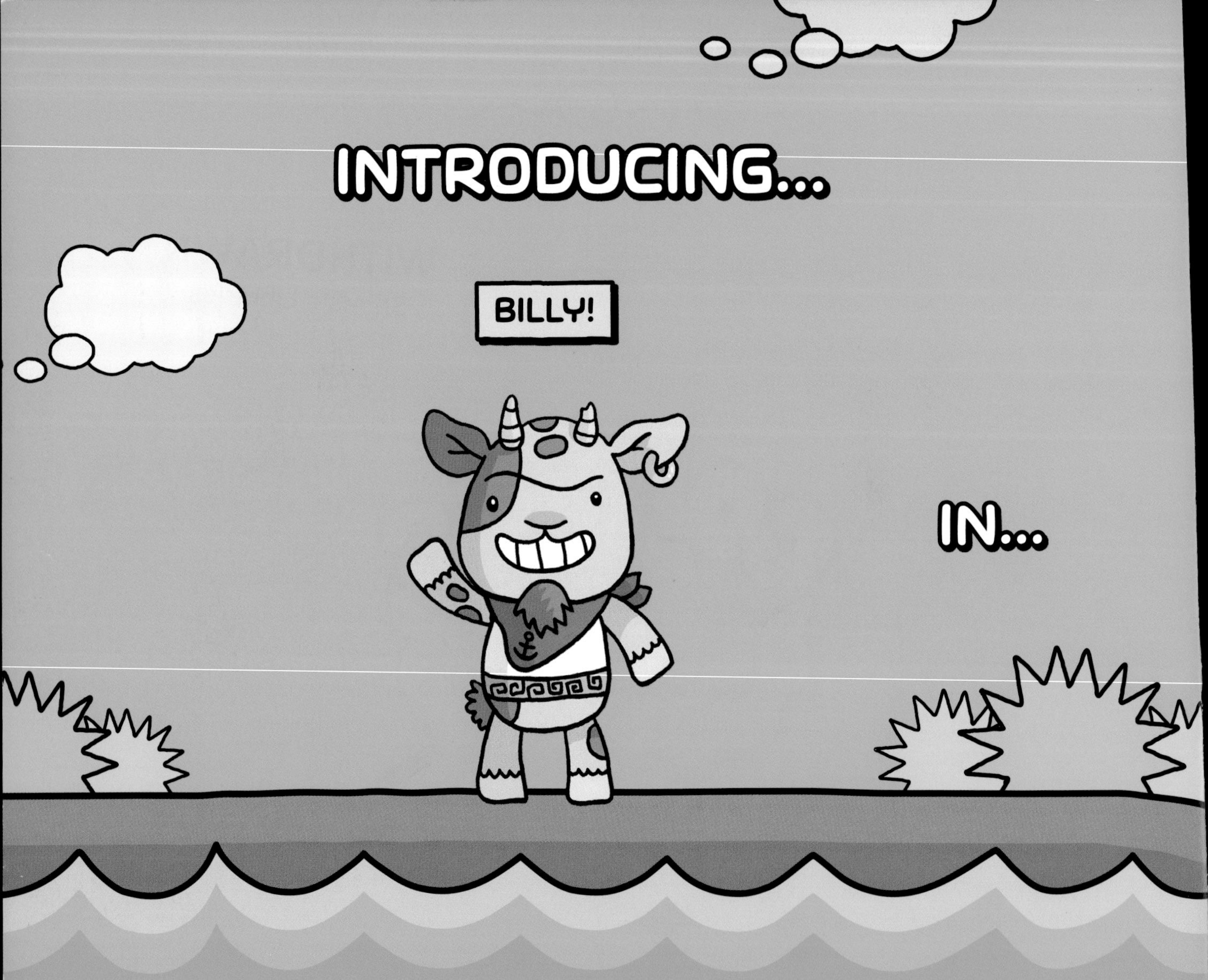
INTRODUCING...
BILLY!
IN...

capstone
www.capstoneyoungreaders.com

1710 Roe Crest Drive, North Mankato, Minnesota 56003



Cataloging-in-Publication data is available on the Library of Congress website.
ISBN: 978-1-4342-6282-0 (hardcover) • ISBN: 978-1-4342-4944-9 (library binding) • ISBN: 978-1-4342-6429-9 (ebook)

Printed in China by Nordica. 0413/CA21300502 032013 007226NORDF13

# GOAT ON A BOAT

written by
**JOHN SAZAKLIS**

illustrated by
**JESS BRADLEY**

designed by
**BOB LENTZ**

edited by
**JULIE GASSMAN**

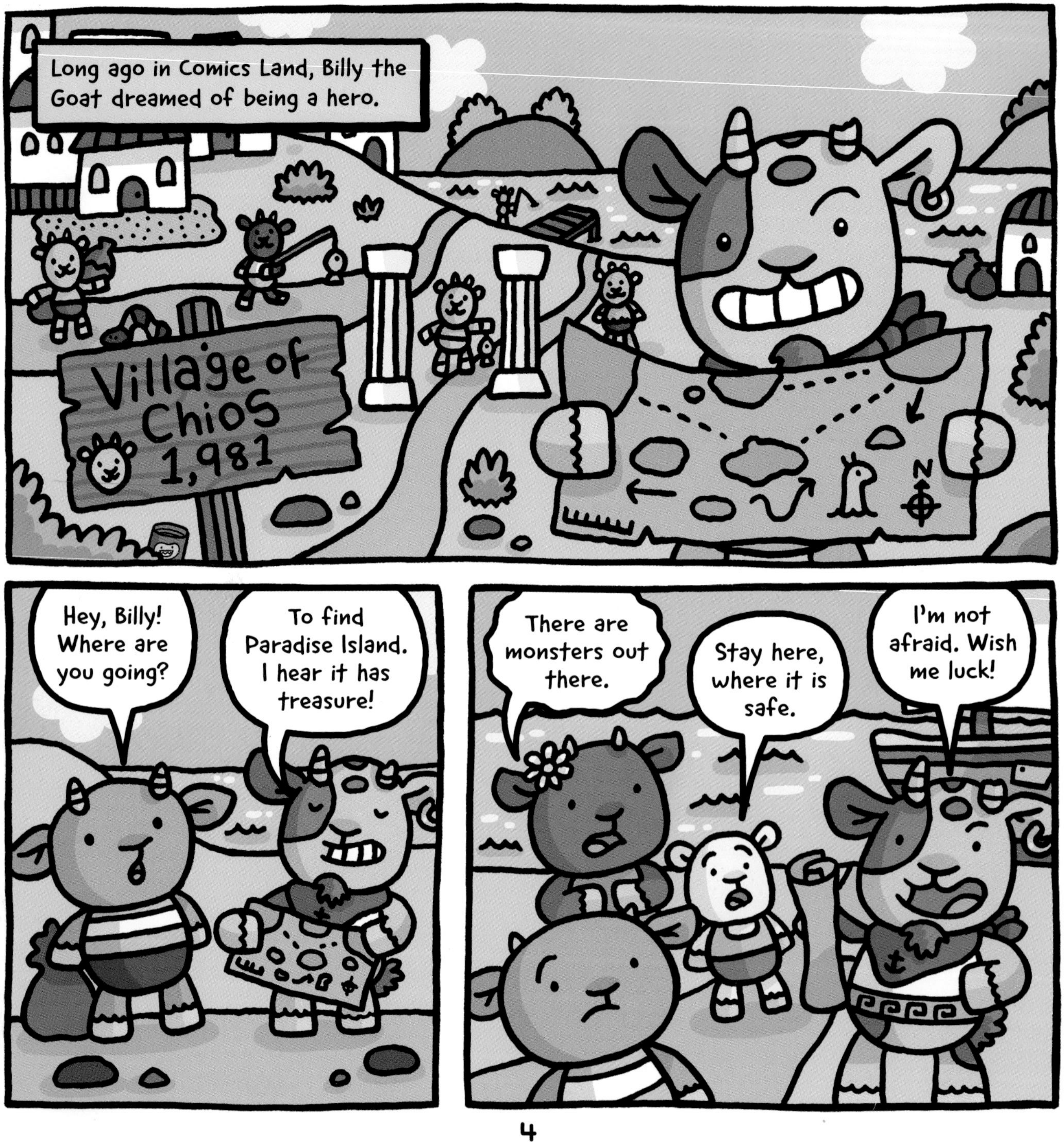
Long ago in Comics Land, Billy the Goat dreamed of being a hero.
Village of Chios 1,981
Hey, Billy! Where are you going?
To find Paradise Island. I hear it has treasure!
There are monsters out there.
Stay here, where it is safe.
I'm not afraid. Wish me luck!

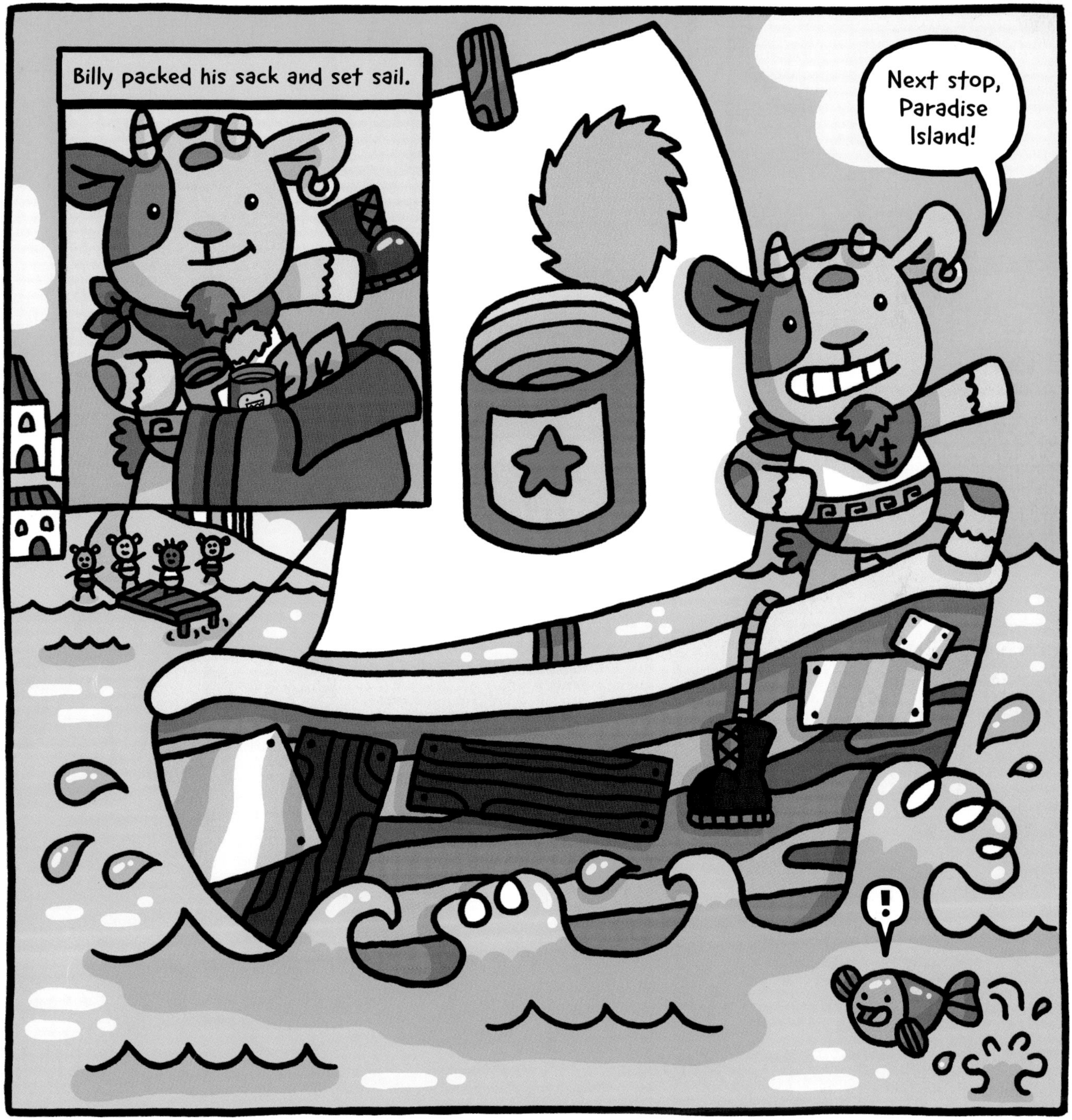
Billy packed his sack and set sail.
Next stop, Paradise Island!
!

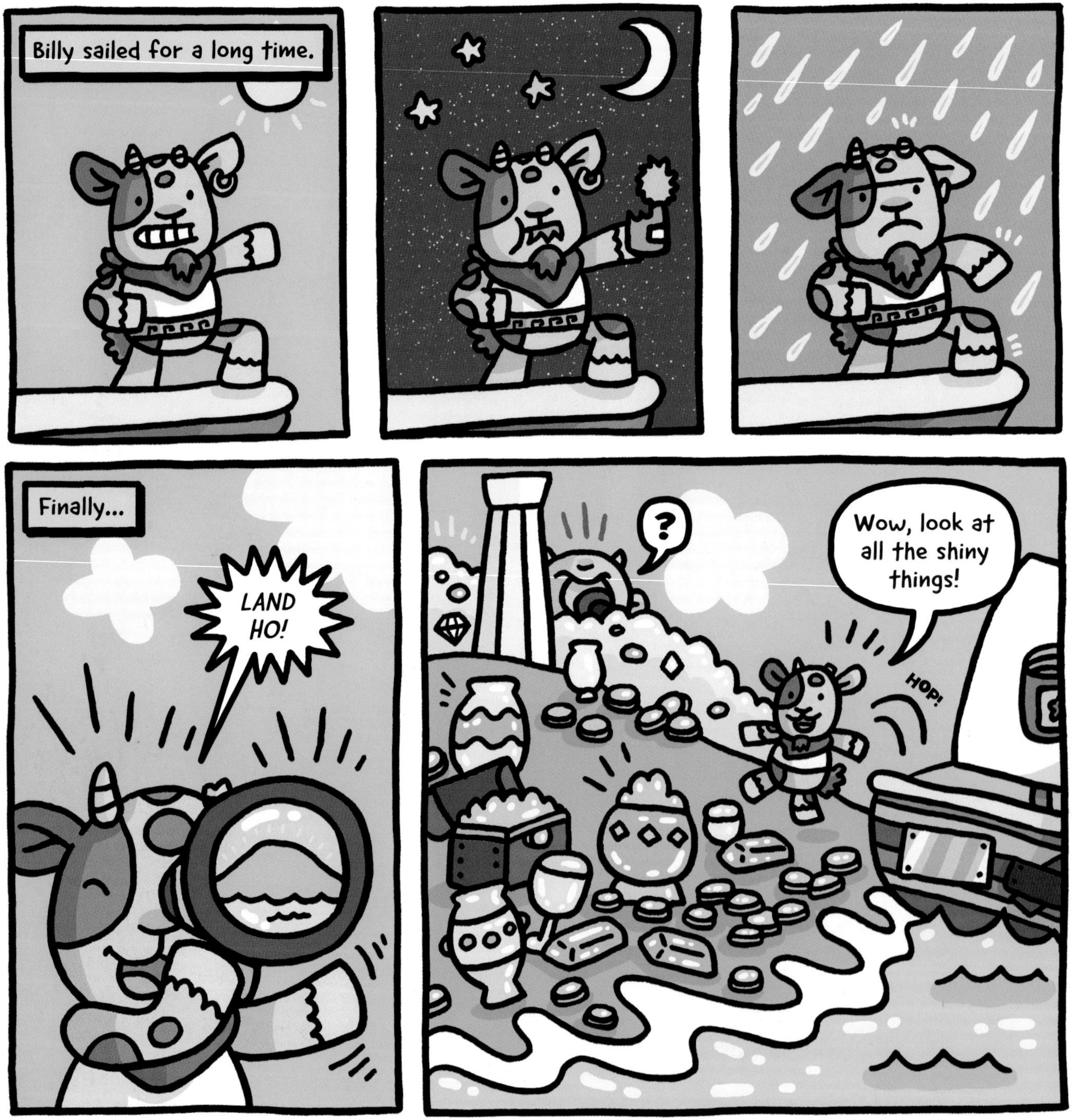
Billy sailed for a long time.
Finally...
LAND HO!
?
Wow, look at all the shiny things!
HOP!

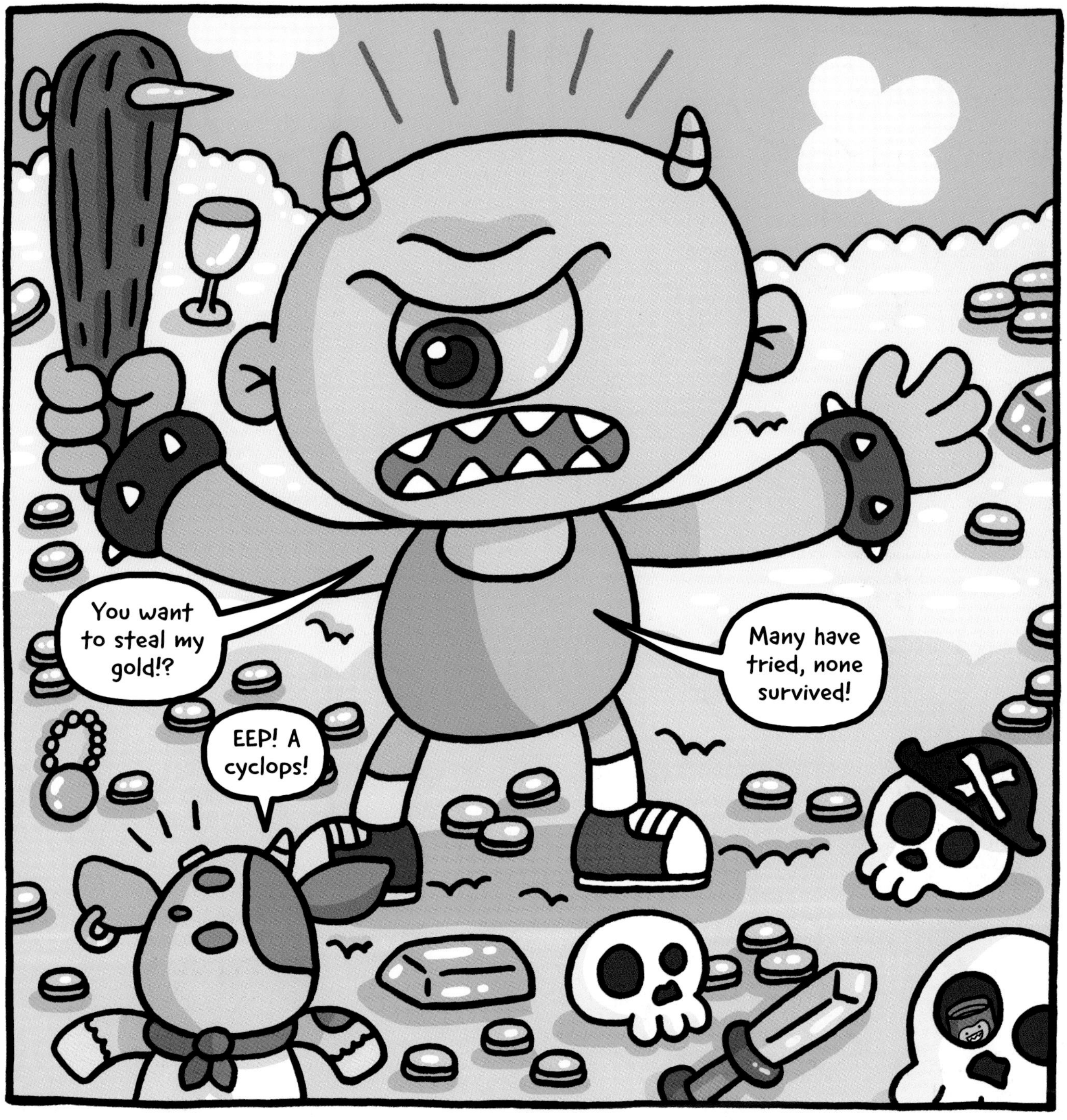
You want to steal my gold!?
Many have tried, none survived!
EEP! A cyclops!

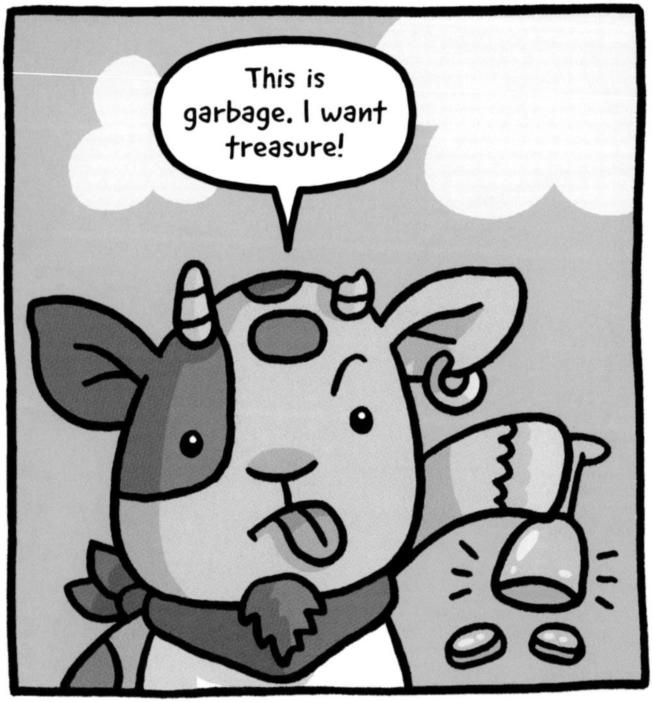
This is garbage. I want treasure!

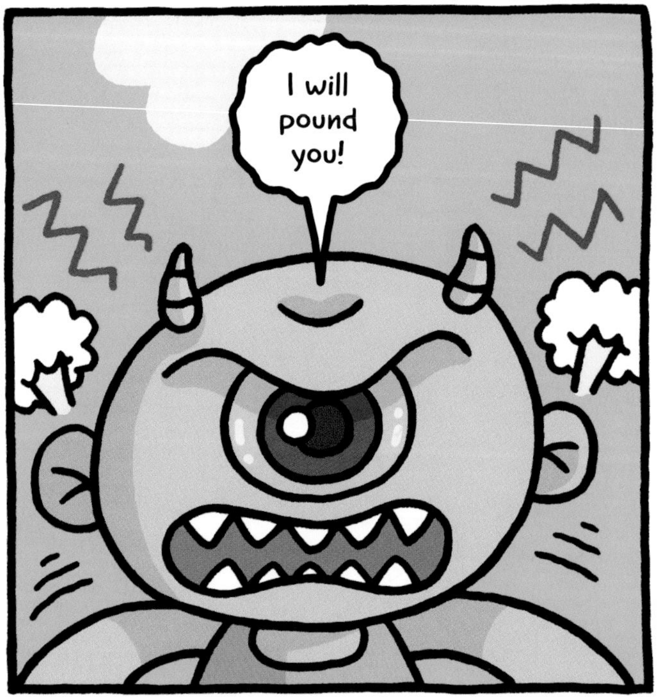
I will pound you!

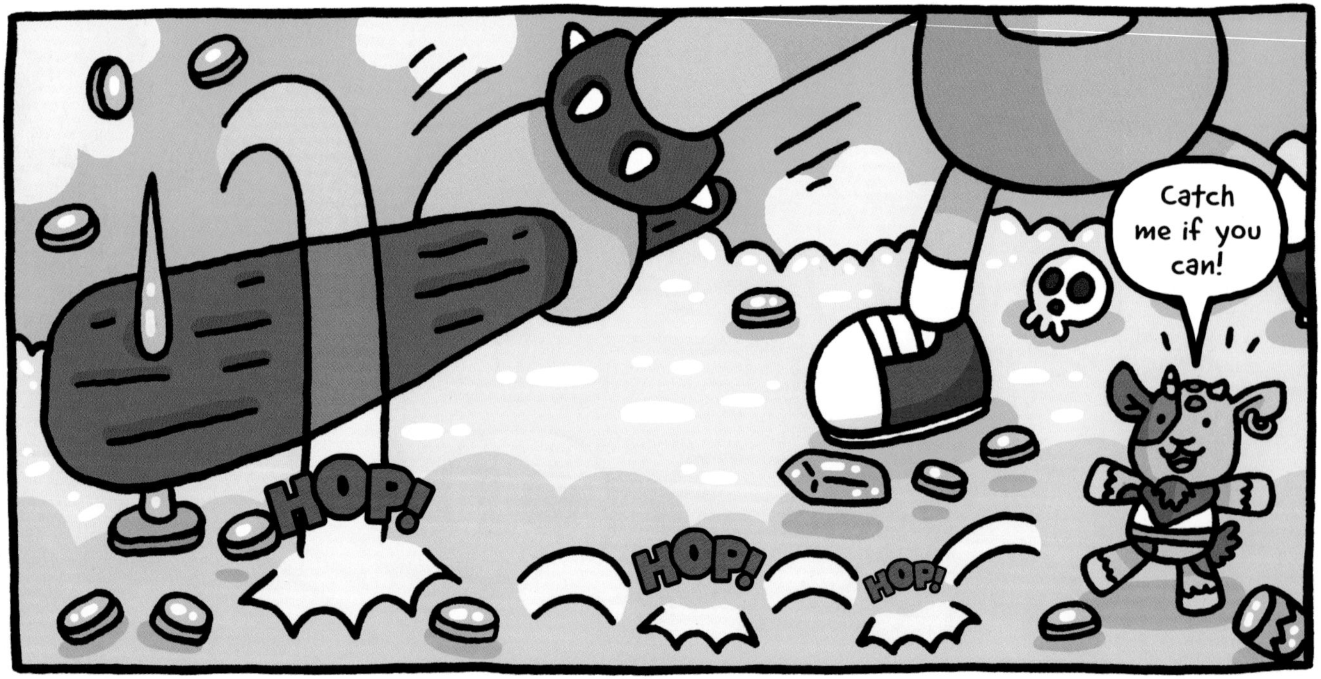
Catch me if you can!
HOP!
HOP!
HOP!

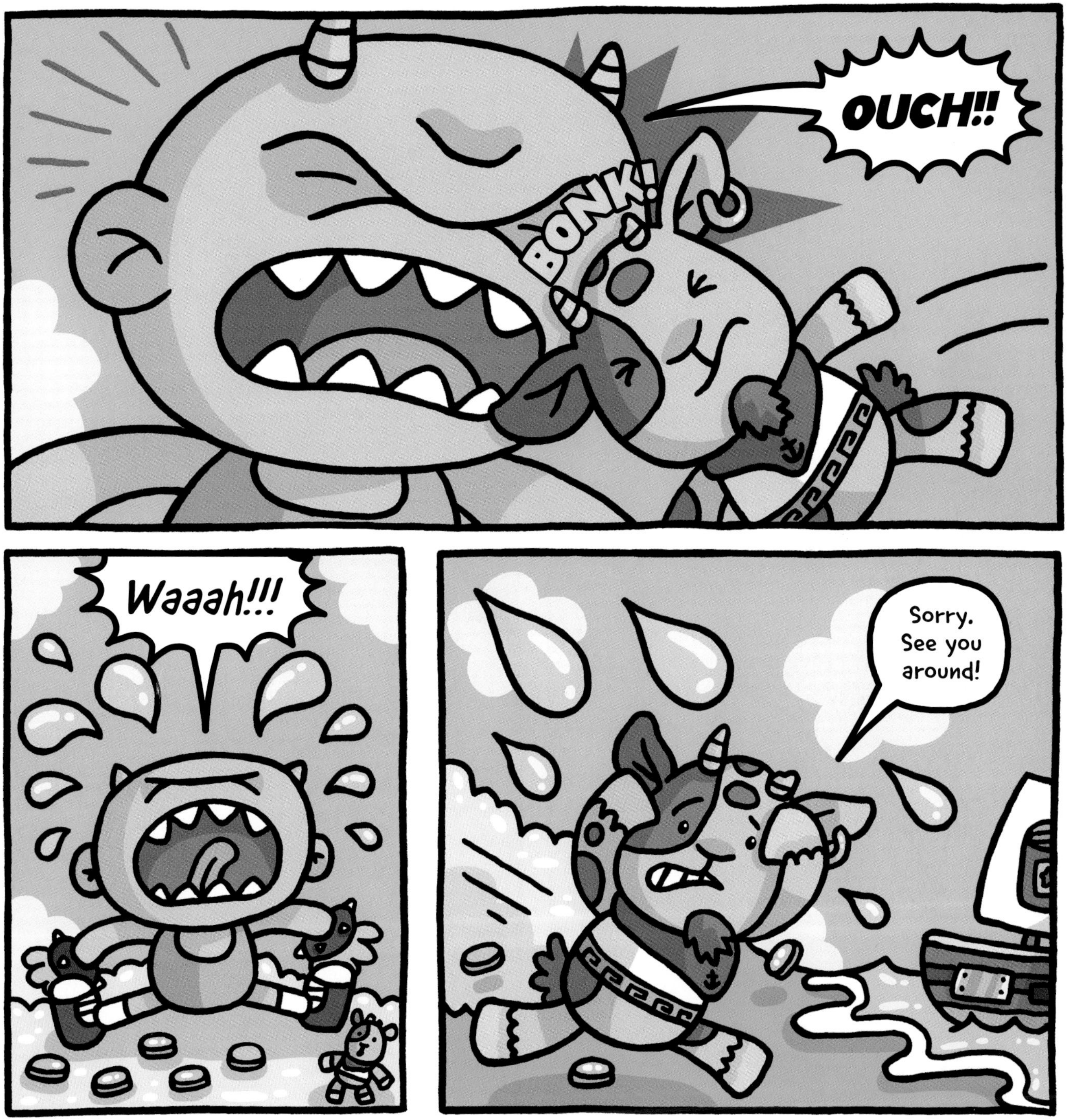
OUCH!!
BONK!
Waaah!!!
Sorry. See you around!

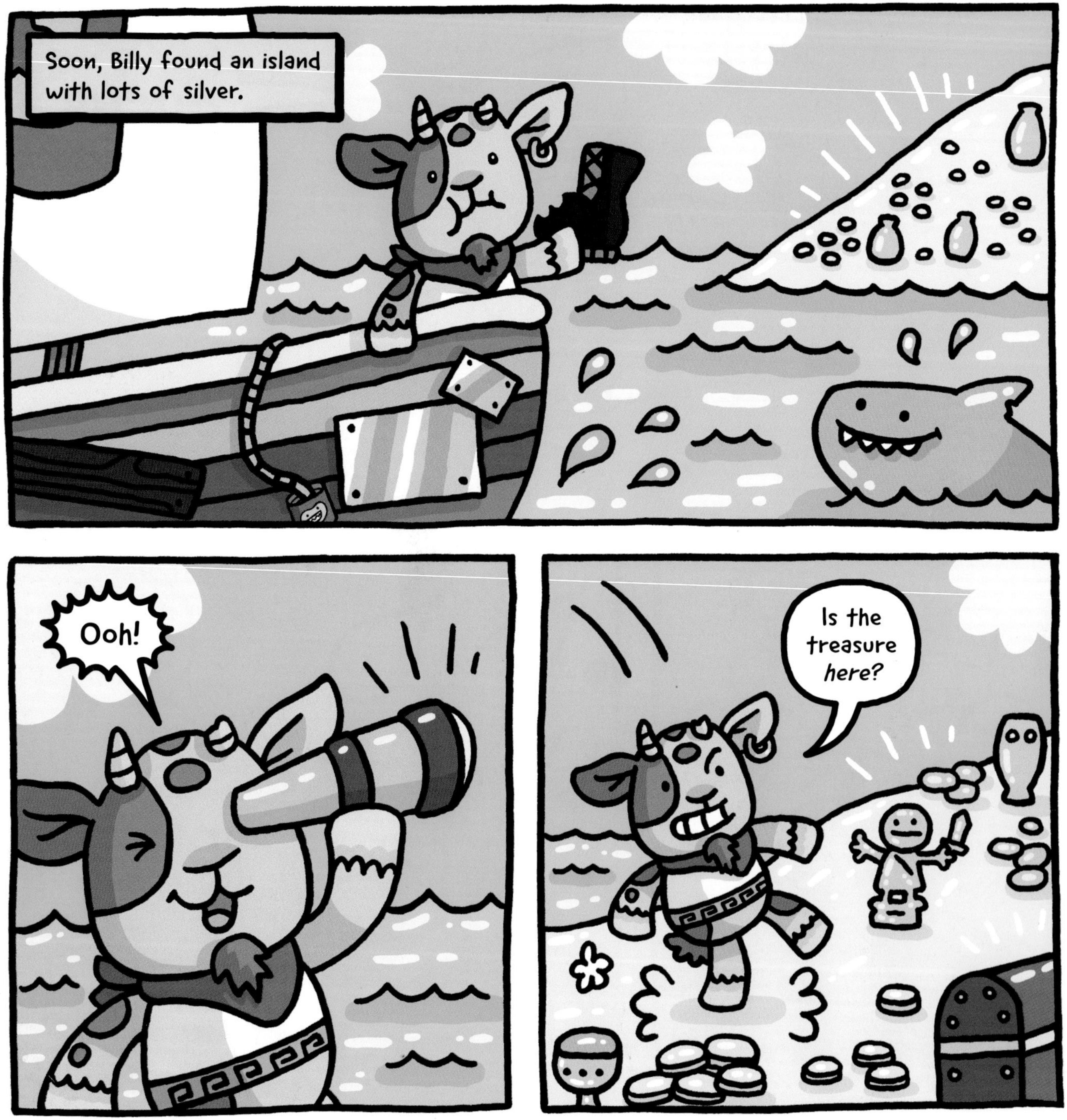

Soon, Billy found an island with lots of silver.
Ooh!
Is the treasure *here*?

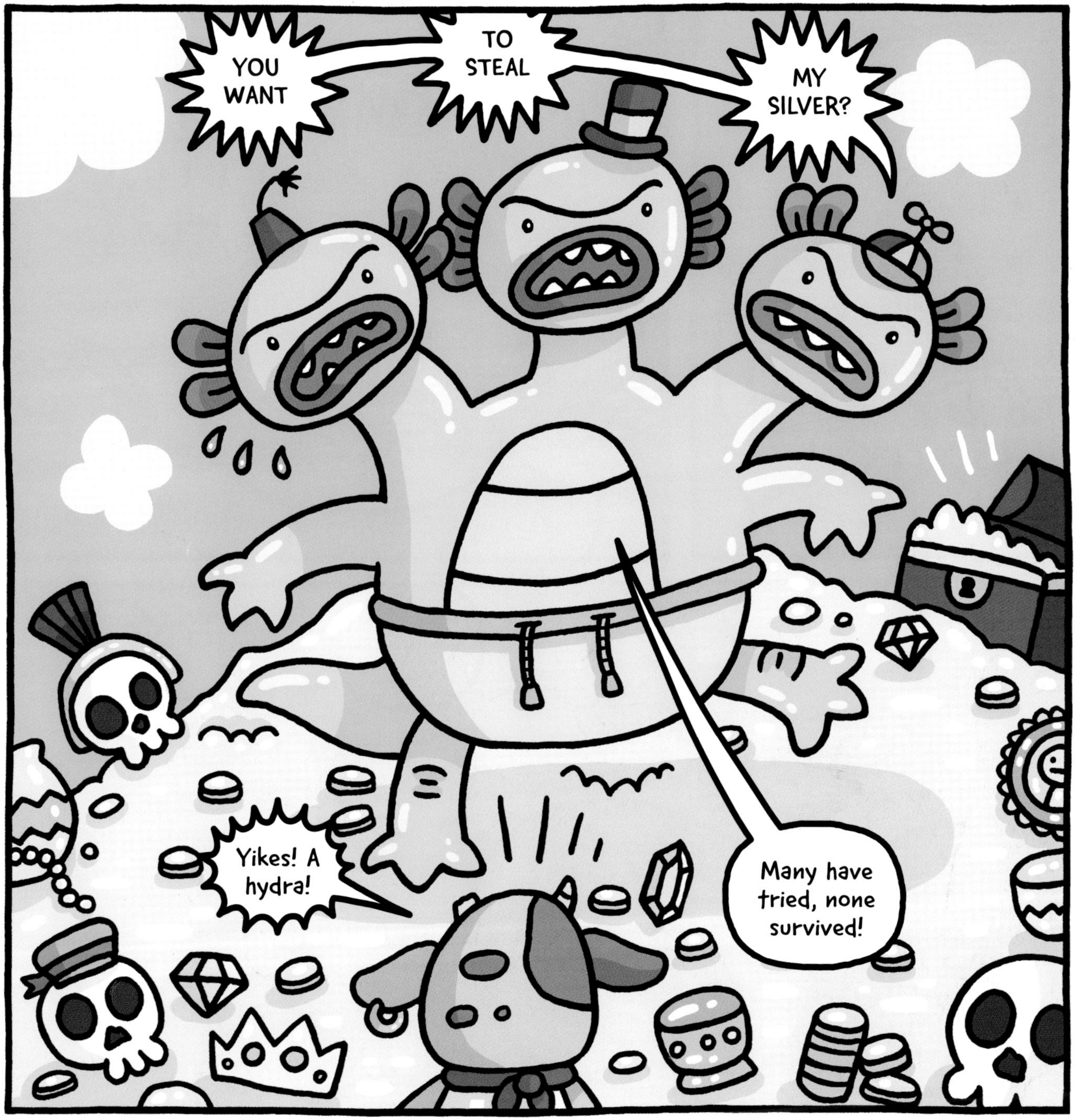
YOU WANT
TO STEAL
MY SILVER?
Yikes! A hydra!
Many have tried, none survived!

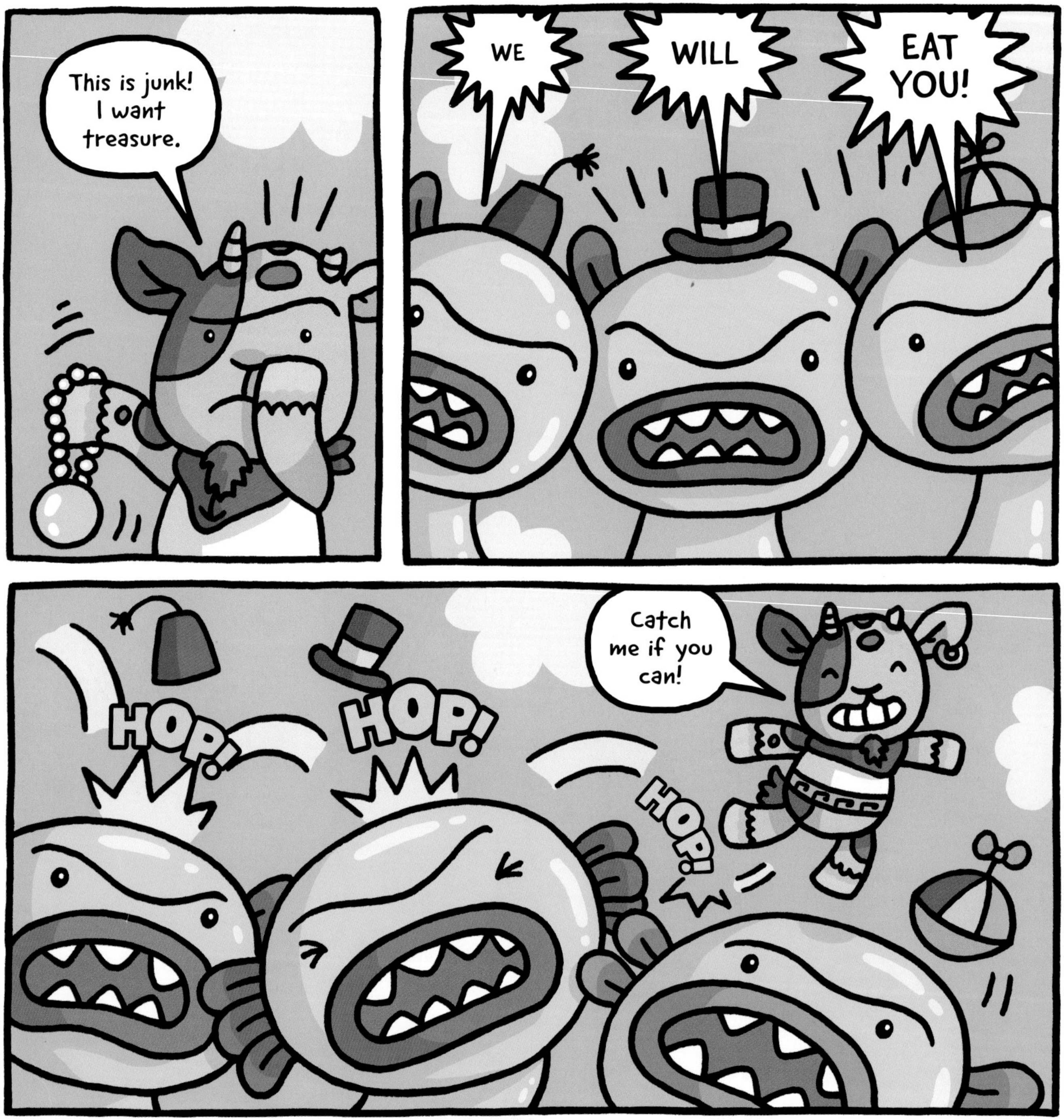
This is junk! I want treasure.
WE
WILL
EAT YOU!
HOP!
HOP!
HOP!
Catch me if you can!

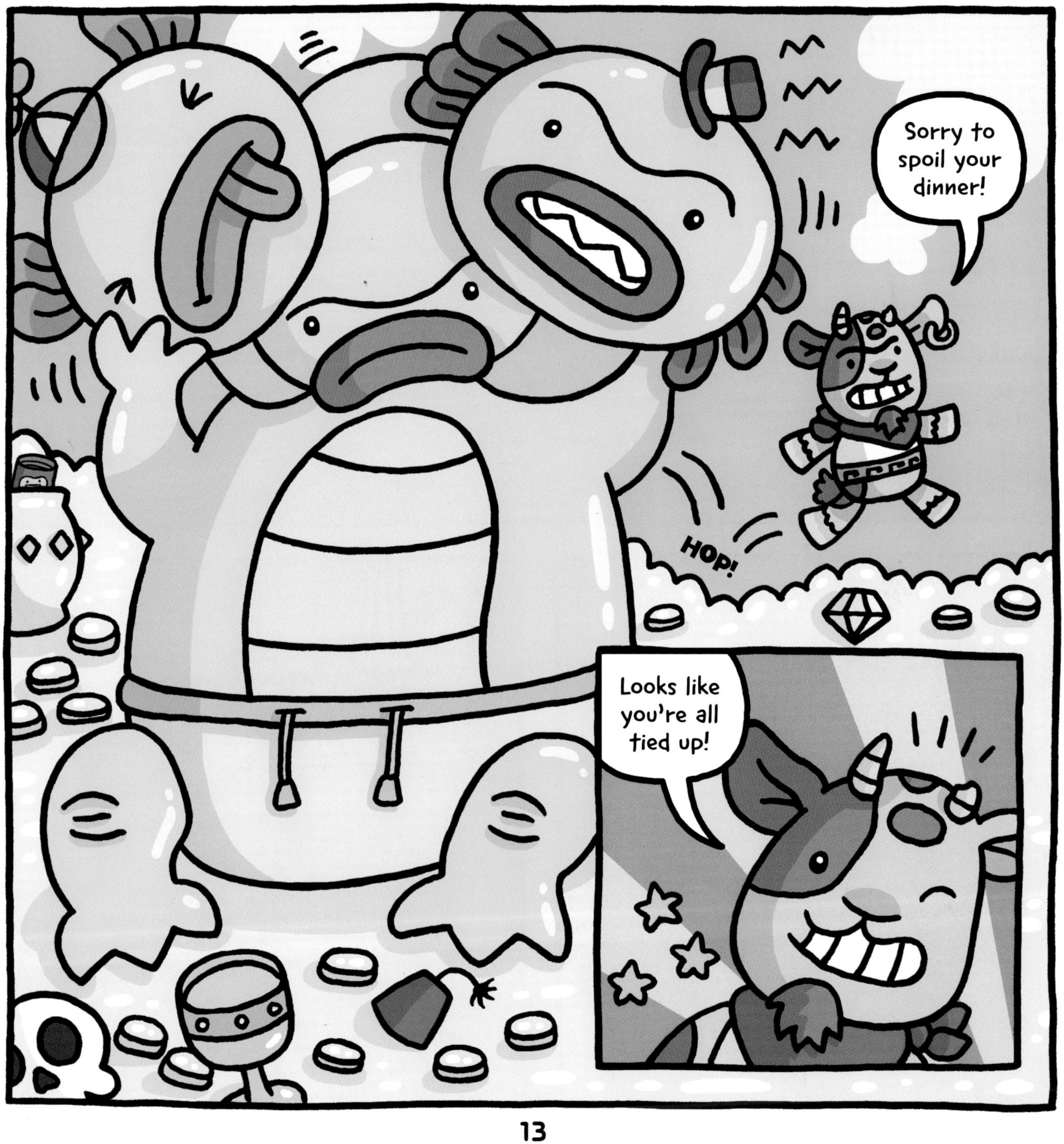
Sorry to spoil your dinner!
HOP!
Looks like you're all tied up!

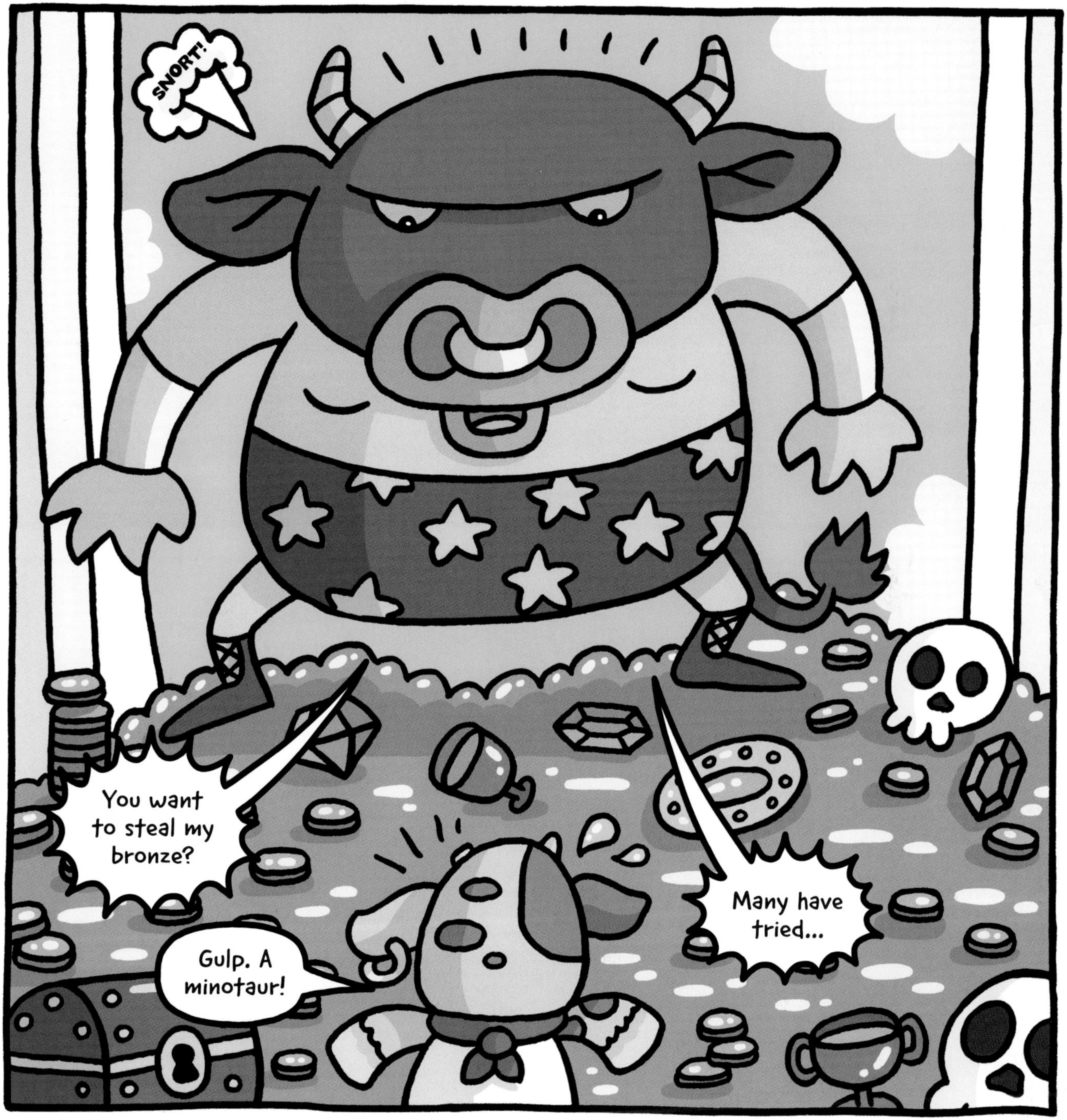
SNORT!
You want to steal my bronze?
Many have tried...
Gulp. A minotaur!

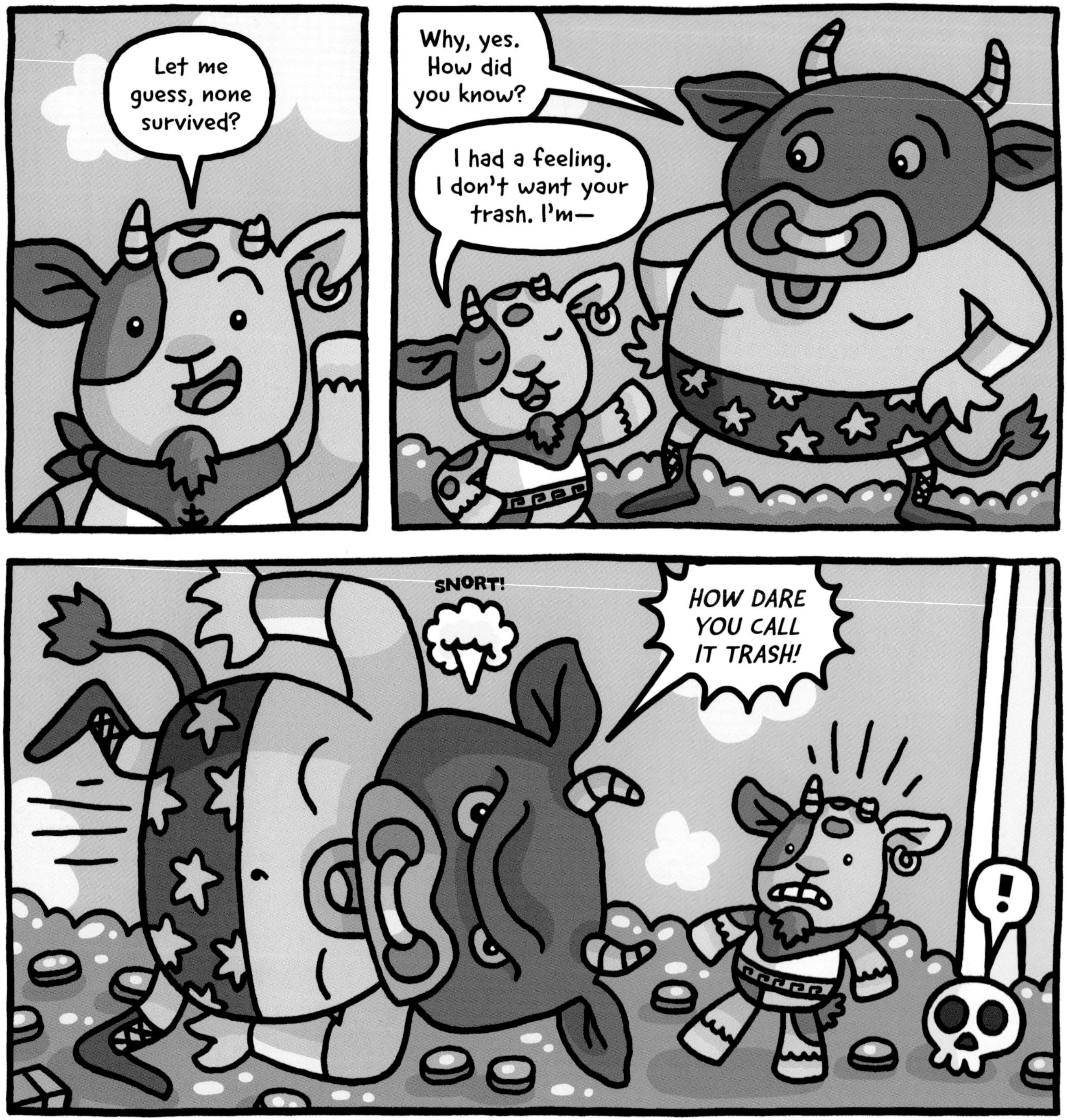
Let me guess, none survived?
Why, yes. How did you know?
I had a feeling. I don't want your trash. I'm—
SNORT!
HOW DARE YOU CALL IT TRASH!
!

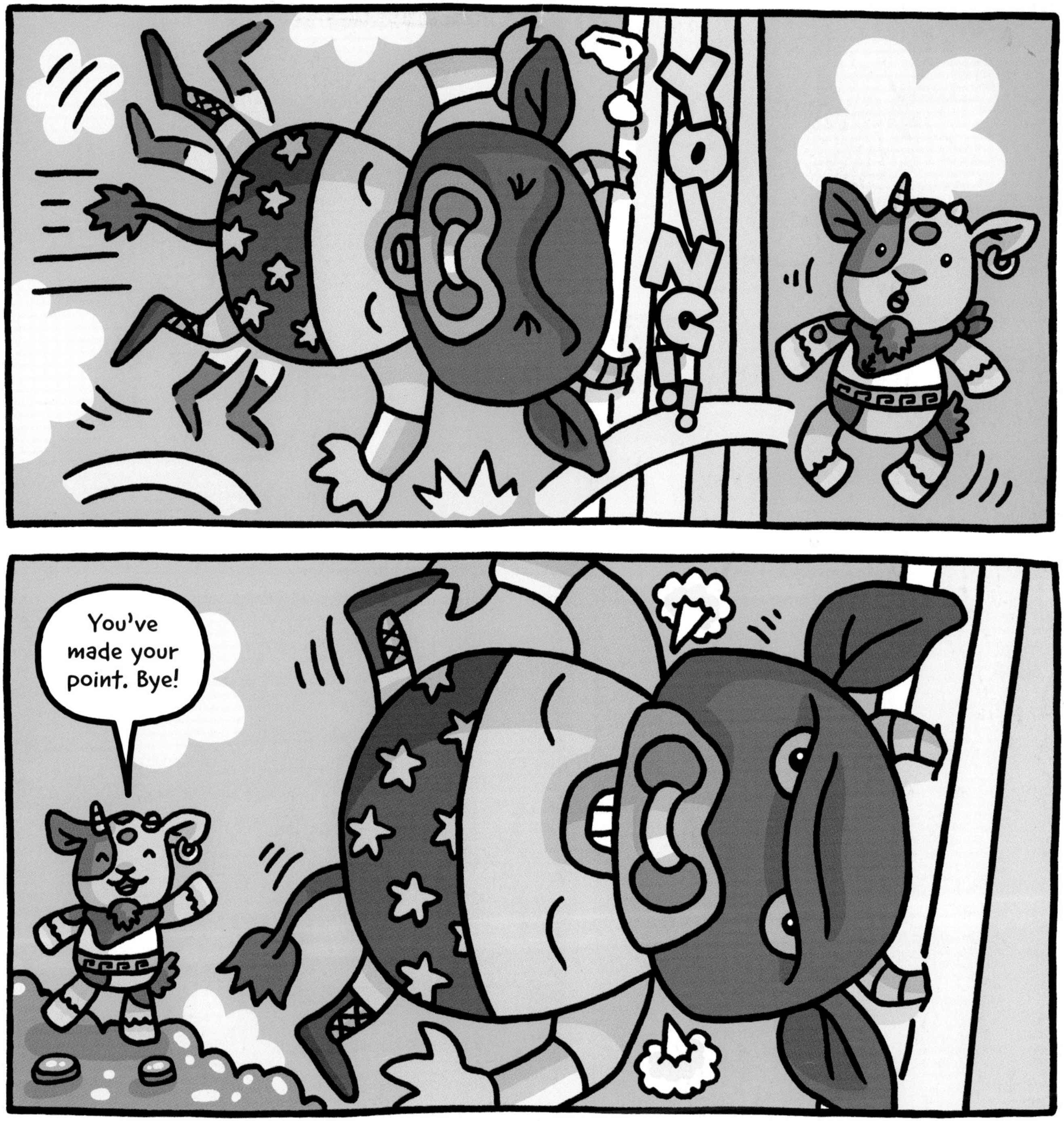
YOING!!
You've made your point. Bye!

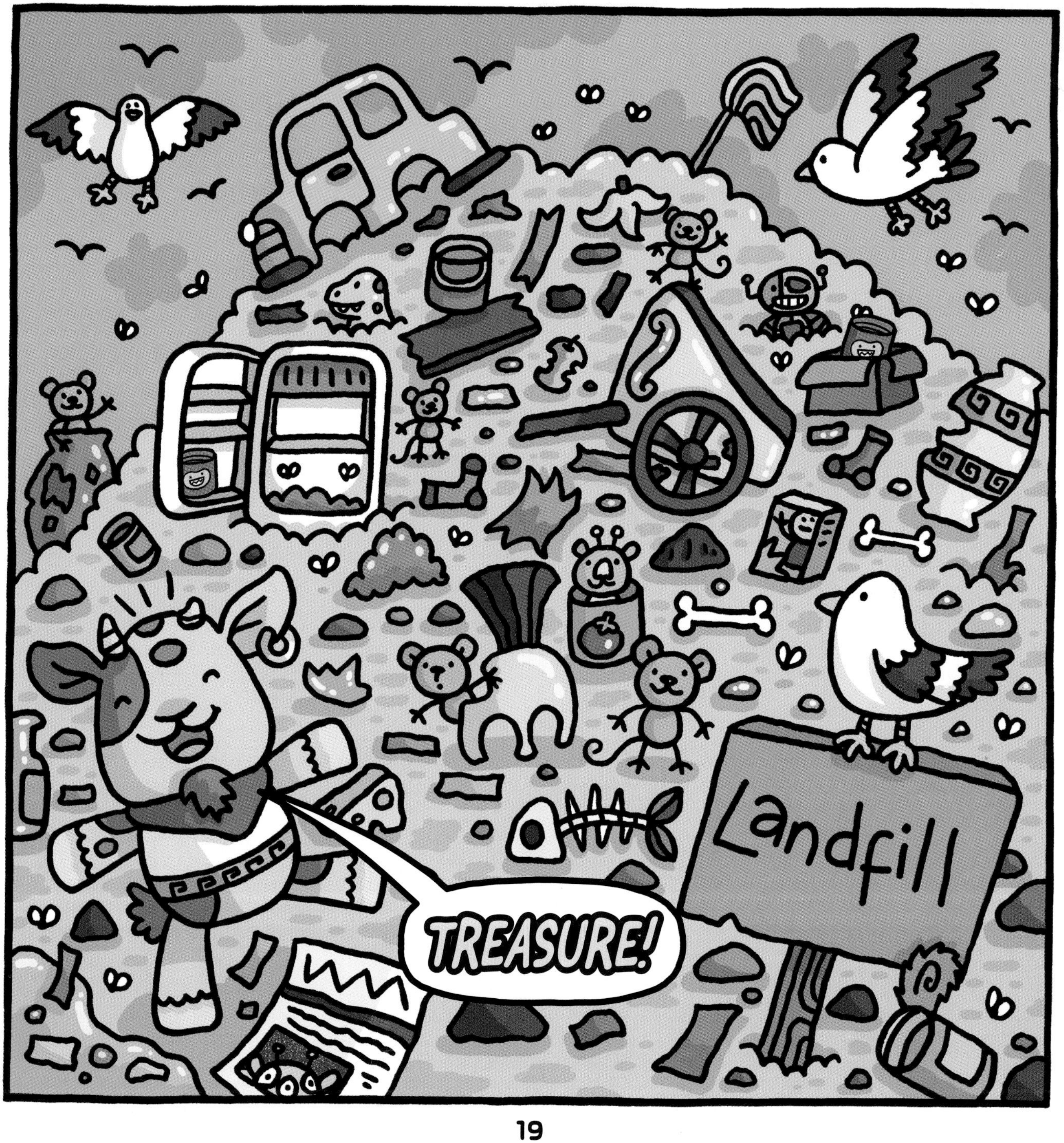
Landfill
TREASURE!

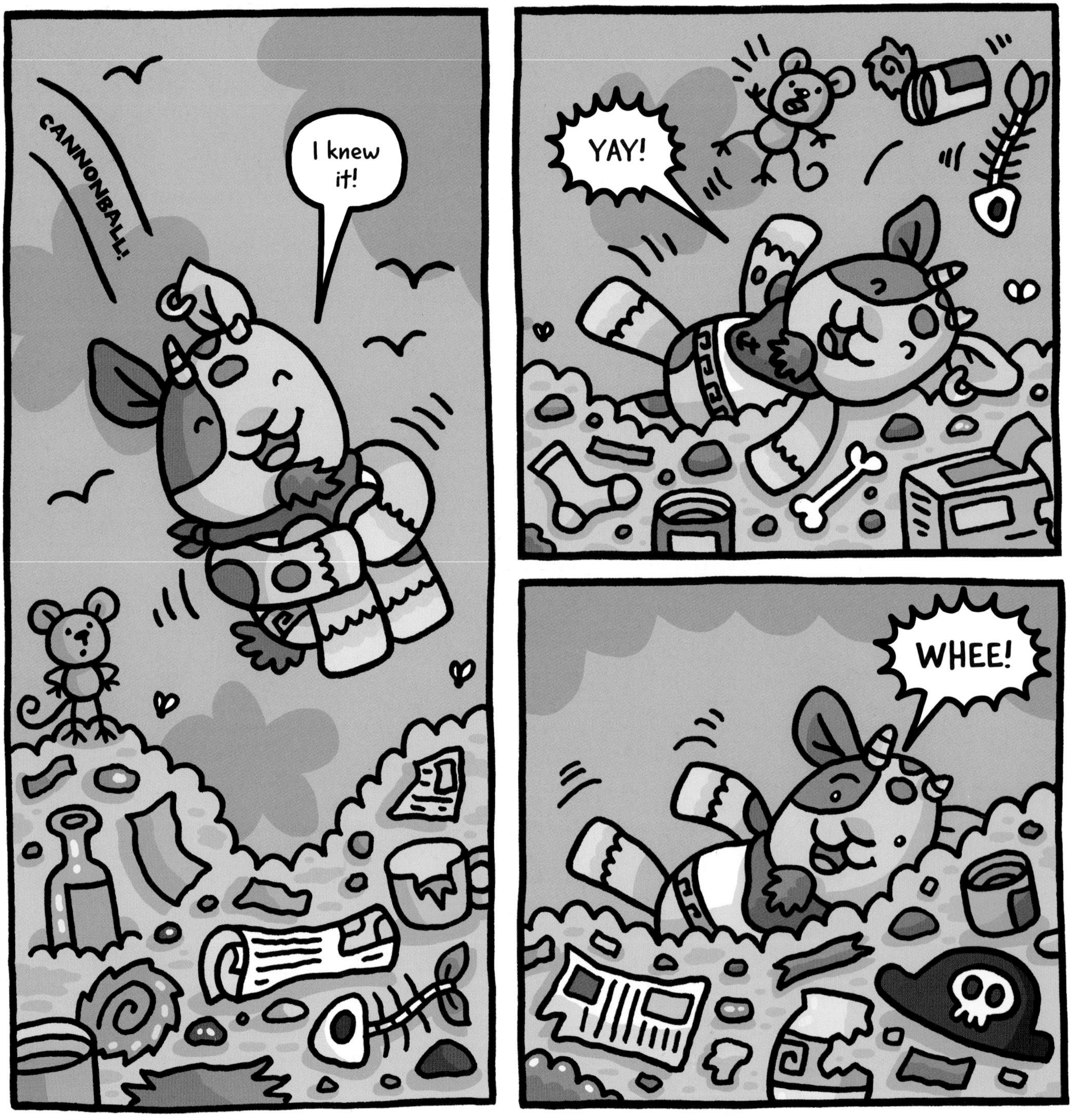
CANNONBALL!
I knew it!
YAY!
WHEE!

22

23

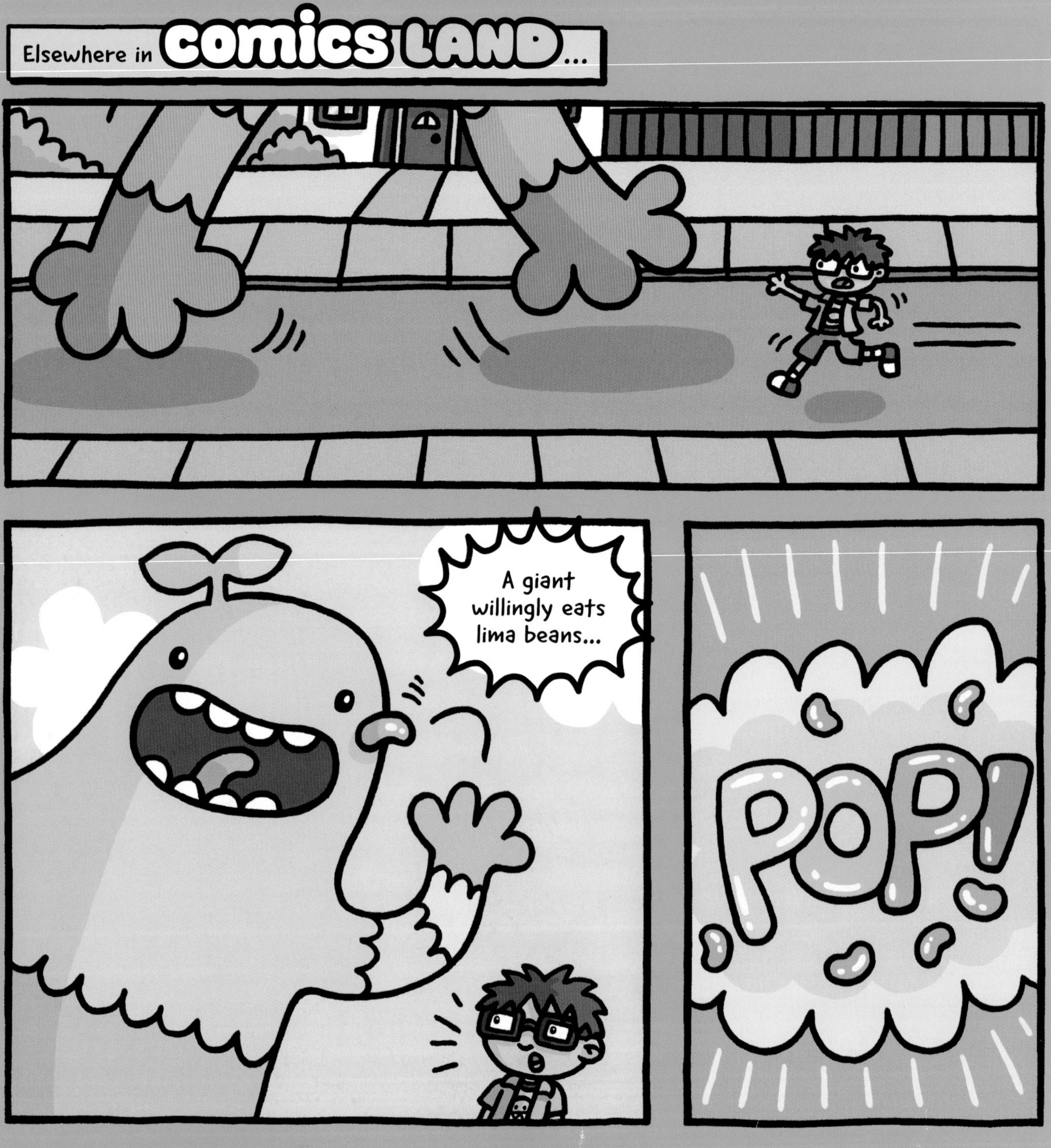
Elsewhere in COMICS LAND...
A giant willingly eats lima beans...
POP!

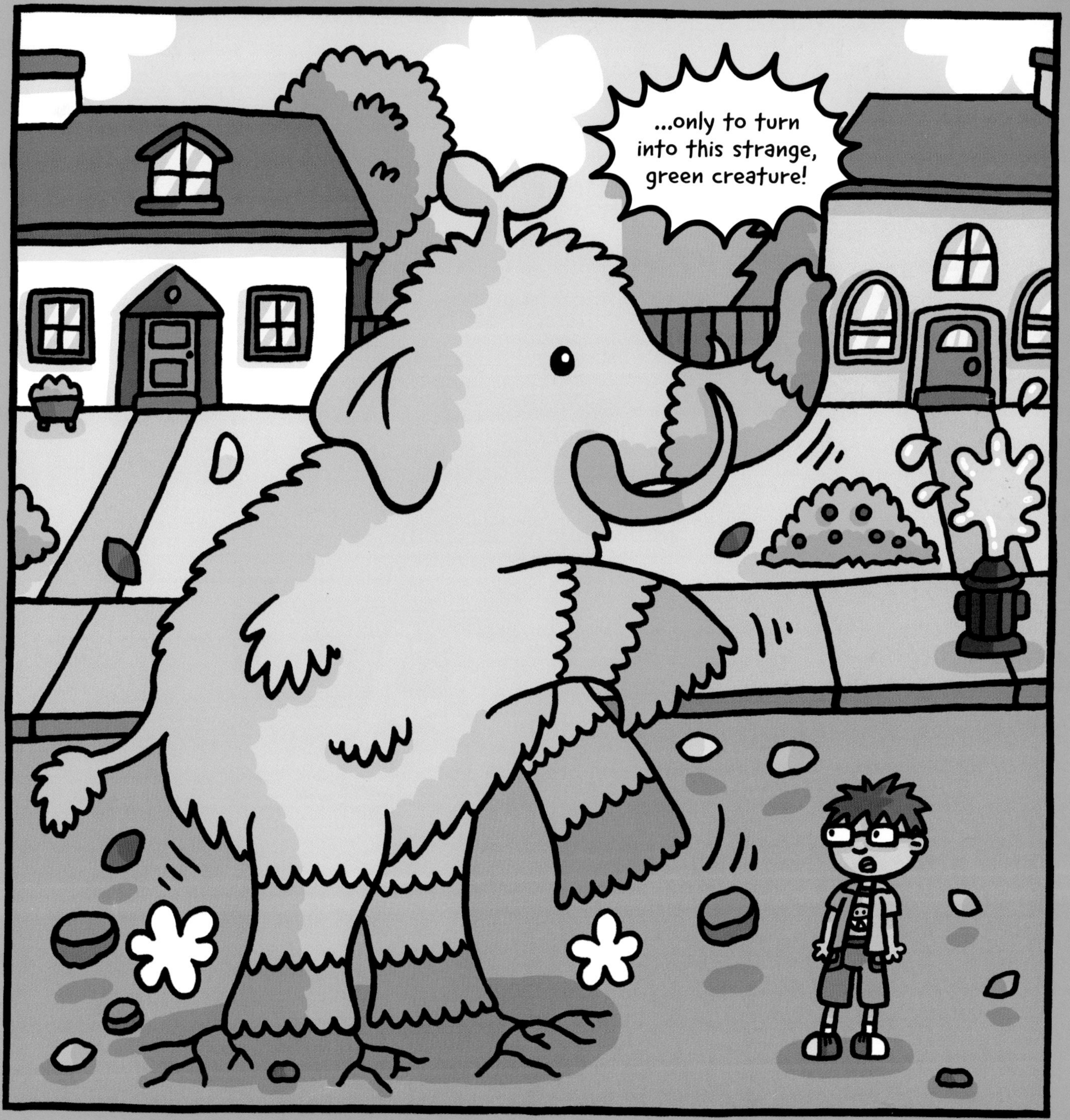
...only to turn into this strange, green creature!

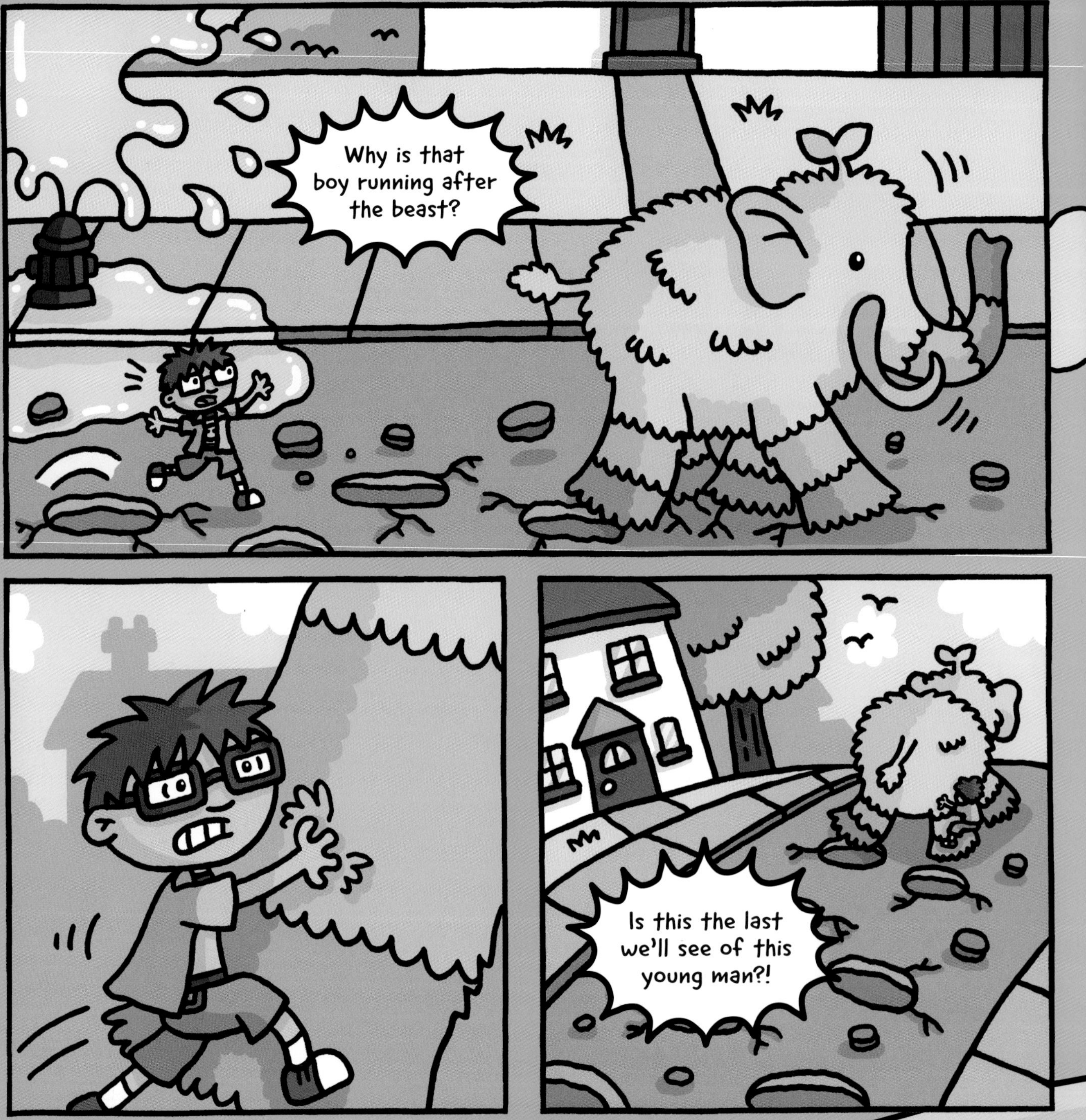
Why is that boy running after the beast?
Is this the last we'll see of this young man?!

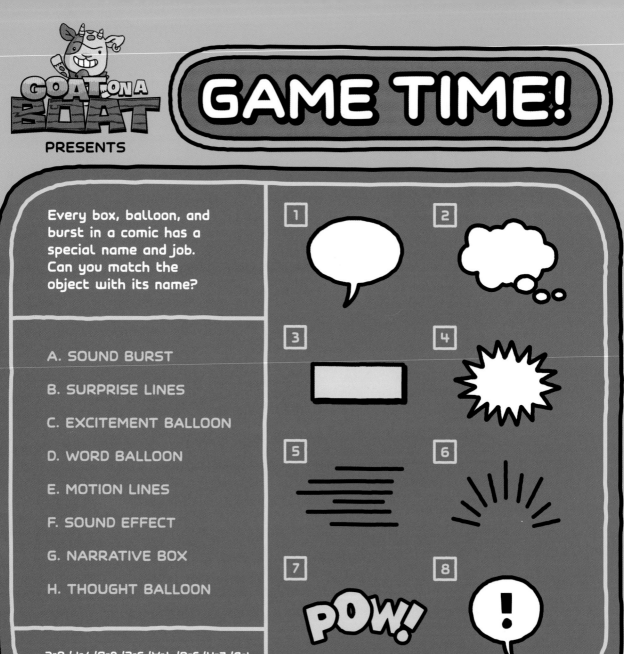

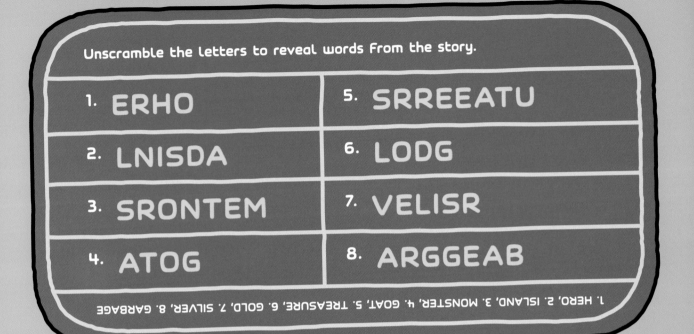

Unscramble the letters to reveal words from the story.

| 1. ERHO | 5. SRREEATU |
| 2. LNISDA | 6. LODG |
| 3. SRONTEM | 7. VELISR |
| 4. ATOG | 8. ARGGEAB |

# FIND THE TIN CAN!

Billy's favorite thing to snack on is red and green cans like this one. Take another look at the story and find the 11 cans hidden throughout the pages.

# DRAW COMICS!

GOAT ON A BOAT PRESENTS

Want to make your own comic about Billy's journey? Start by learning to draw the little goat. Comics Land artist Jess Bradley shows you how in six easy steps!

You will need:

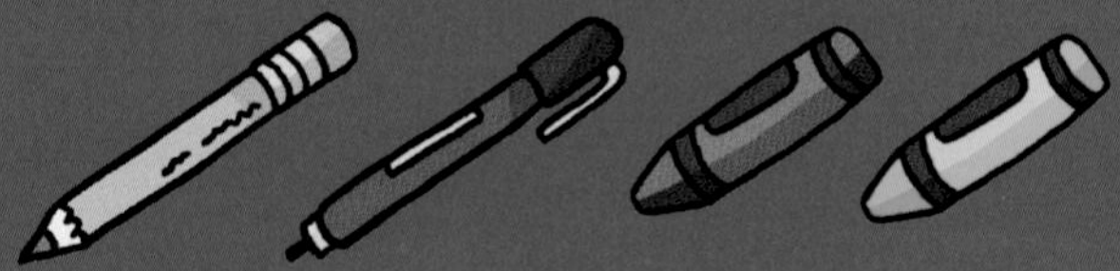

1.

2.

Draw in pencil!

**3.**

**4.**

**5.**

Outline in ink!

**6.**

Color!

# JOHN SAZAKLIS

## AUTHOR

John Sazaklis spent part of life working in a family coffee shop, the House of Donuts. The other part, he spent drawing and writing stories. He has illustrated Spider-Man books and written Batman books for HarperCollins. He has also created toys used in *MAD Magazine*.

# JESS BRADLEY

## ARTIST

Jess Bradley is an illustrator living and working in Bristol, England. She likes playing video games, painting, and watching bad films. Jess can also be heard to make a high-pitched "squeeeee" when excited, usually while watching videos clips of otters or getting new comics in the mail.

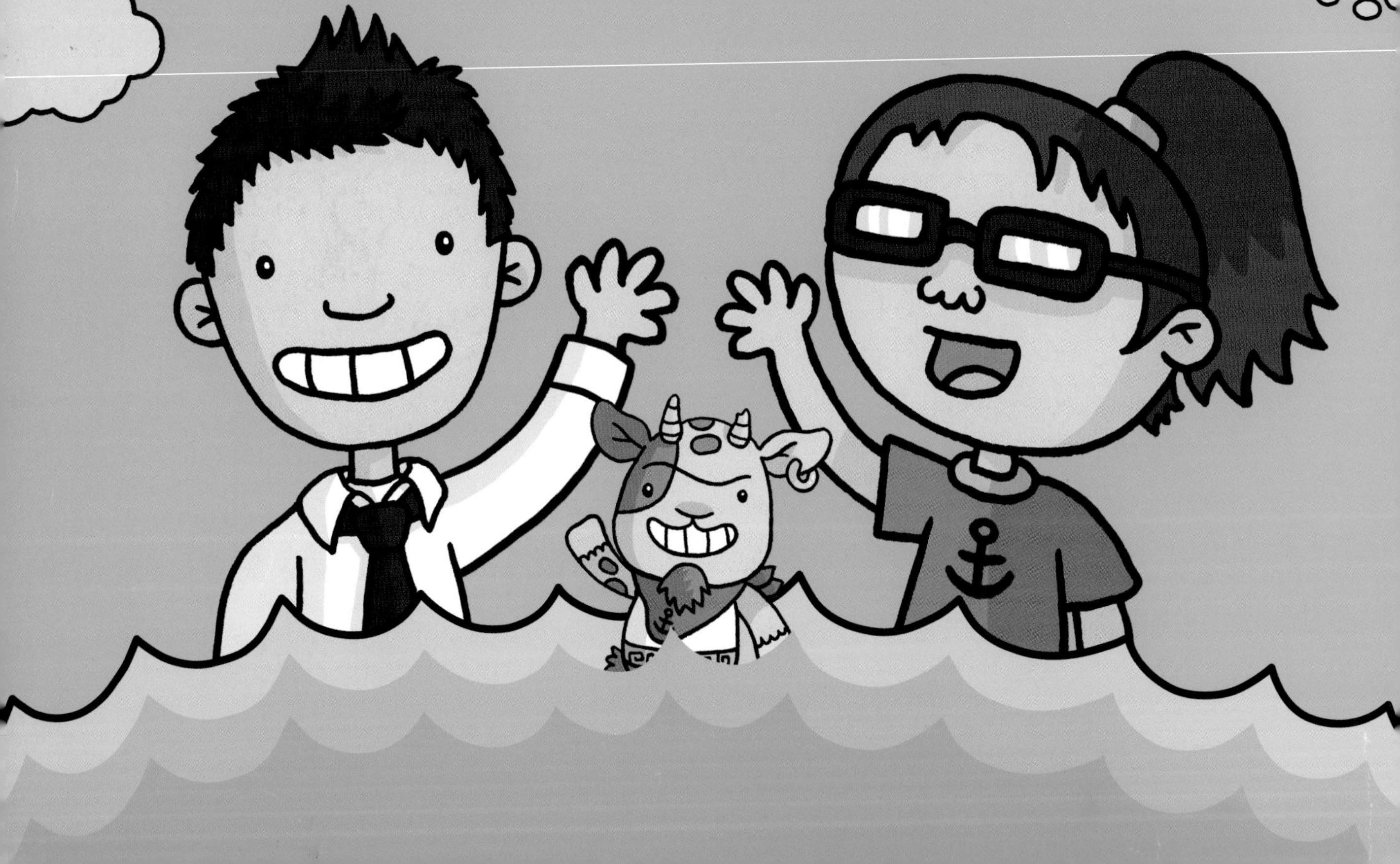

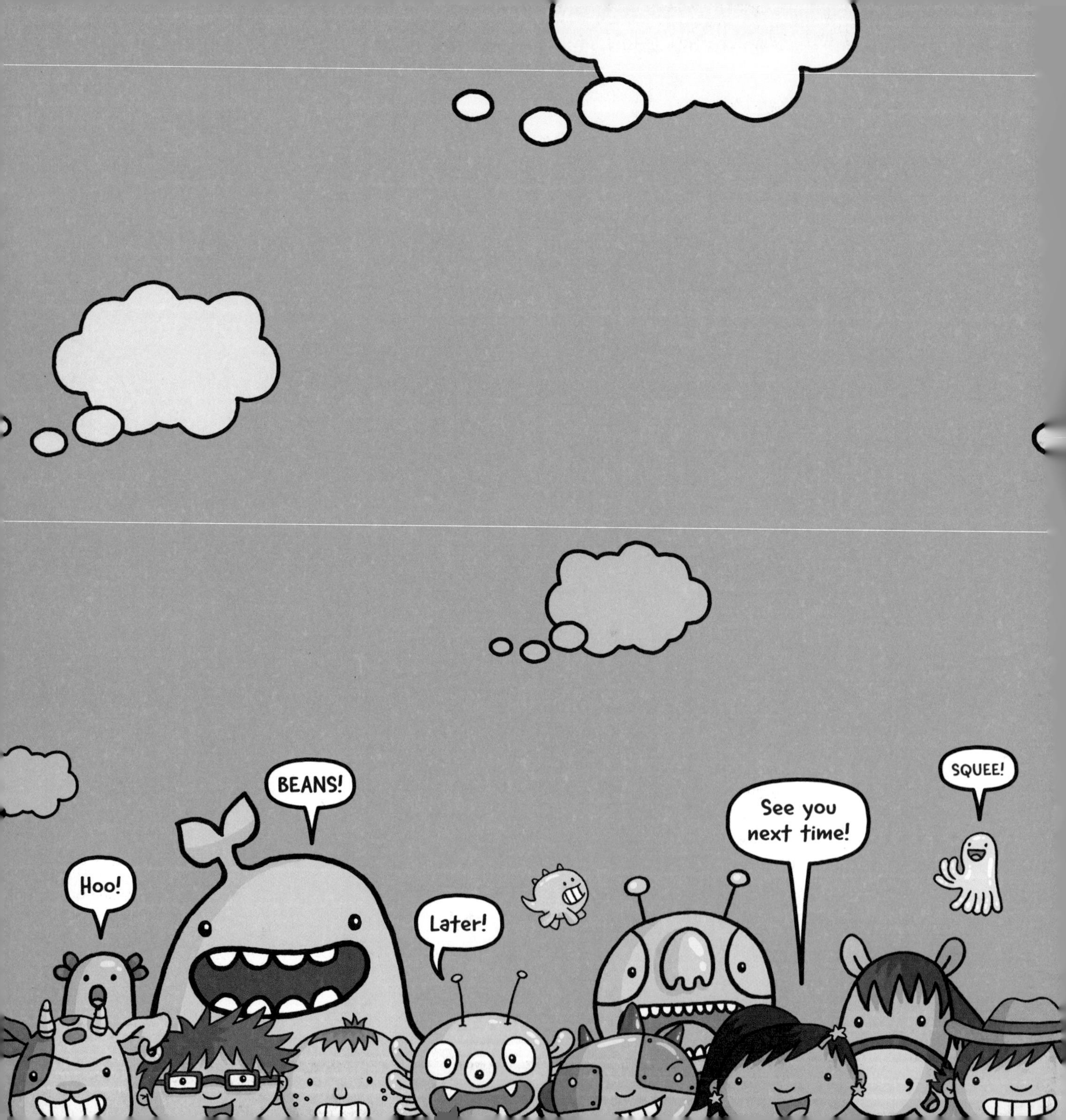
Hoo!
BEANS!
Later!
See you next time!
SQUEE!